BUFFALO WOMAN

BUFFALO WOMAN

Story and illustrations by PAUL GOBLE

Bradbury Press — New York

for Marco

The story of *Buffalo Woman* comes from the tribes who followed the buffalo herds on the Great Plains. The buffalo was the source of life for the people, giving them food, hides for robes and tipi covers, as well as many other things. The lives of both were closely interwoven, and the story teaches that buffalo and people were related. The stories varied from tribe to tribe, but this deep sense of kinship with the buffalo was the same for the Blackfeet living in the north (Montana), as it was for the Comanche in the south (Texas). These stories were not simply for entertainment; they had power to strengthen the bond with the herds, and to encourage the herds to continue to give themselves so that the people could live. It was felt that retelling the story had power to bring about a change within each of us; that in listening we might all be a little more worthy of our buffalo relatives.

REFERENCES: George A. Dorsey, THE BUFFALO WIFE AND THE JAVELIN GAME—Traditions of the Arikara, Carnegie Institute, Washington, DC, 1904; THE MAN WHO MARRIED A BUFFALO—The Pawnee Mythology (Part 1), Carnegie Institute, Washington, DC, 1906; YOUNG-BOY-CHIEF, WHO MARRIED A BUFFALO—The Mythology of the Wichita, Carnegie Institute, Washington, DC, 1904; THE MAN WHO MARRIED A BUFFALO—Traditions of the Skidi Pawnee, American Folk-lore Society, Boston, 1904; George Bird Grinnell, THE BUFFALO WIFE—By Cheyenne Campfires, Yale University Press, New Haven, 1926; Robert H. Lowie, THE BUFFALO WIFE—Myths and Traditions of the Crow Indians, American Museum of Natural History, Vol XXV Part 1, New York, 1918; S.C. Simms, OLD MAN COYOTE, THE MAN AND THE COW BUFFALO AND COW ELK—Traditions of the Crows, Field Columbian Museum, Vol 2 #6, Chicago, 1903; John Stands In Timber, THE GREAT RACE—Cheyenne Memories, Yale University Press, New Haven, 1967; Gene Weltfish, THE MAN WHO MARRIED A BUFFALO WIFE—Caddoan Texts, American Ethnological Society, XVII, New York, 1937; Clark Wissler and D.C. Duvall, THE HORNS OF THE MATOKE—Mythology of the Blackfoot Indians, American Museum of Natural History, New York, 1908.

Bradbury Press
866 Third Ave., New York, NY 10022
An affiliate of Macmillan, Inc.
Collier Macmillan Canada, Inc.
Manufactured in the United States of America
10 9 8 7 6
The text of this book is set in 14 pt. Baskerville. The illustrations are India ink and watercolor, reproduced in combined line and halftone.
Library of Congress Cataloging in Publication Data
Goble, Paul.
Buffalo woman.
Summary: A young hunter marries a female buffalo in the form of a beautiful maiden, but when his people reject her he must pass several tests before being allowed to join the buffalo nation.
    1. Indians of North America—Legends [1. Indians of North America—Legends. 2. Buffaloes—Fiction]
I. Title.
E98.F6G62 1984   398.2'45297358   83-15704
ISBN 0-02-737720-2

There was a young man who was already a great hunter. Even coyotes and the crows and magpies followed him to pick up the scraps from his hunting. He felt a wonderful harmony with the buffalo. The people knew he could find the herds when they needed meat. When they had hunted, the young man gave thanks that the buffalo had offered themselves.

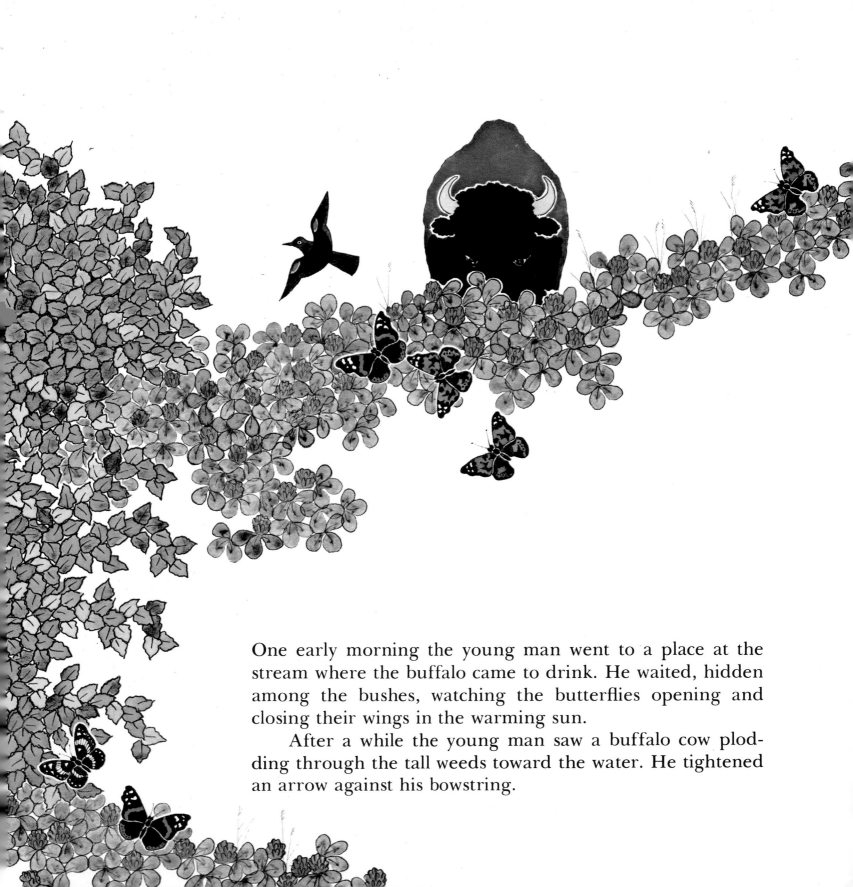

One early morning the young man went to a place at the stream where the buffalo came to drink. He waited, hidden among the bushes, watching the butterflies opening and closing their wings in the warming sun.

After a while the young man saw a buffalo cow plodding through the tall weeds toward the water. He tightened an arrow against his bowstring.

The buffalo was coming very slowly.

The young man did not know whether he fell asleep, or what happened, but when he looked again the buffalo was not there. Instead, a beautiful young woman stepped from the weeds onto the pebbles at the water's edge and took a drink. She was not one of his people; her clothes were different and her hair was not braided. She smelled of wild sage and prairie flowers. He knew at once that he loved her.

"I come from the Buffalo Nation," she told him. "They have sent me because you have always had good feelings for our people. They know you are a good and kind man. I will be your wife. My people wish that the love we have for each other will be an example to both our peoples to follow."

The young man and the beautiful young woman were married. They had a son and named him Calf Boy. Their life together was good.

But the young man's relatives did not like his wife. They often said unkind things among themselves: "He has married a woman without a family," they said. "Her ways are different; she's like an animal. She will never be one of our family."

One day when the young man was away hunting, his relatives came and said to his wife: "You should never have come here; go back to wherever you came from. You are nothing but an animal, anyway." At that she immediately picked up Calf Boy and ran out of the tipi.

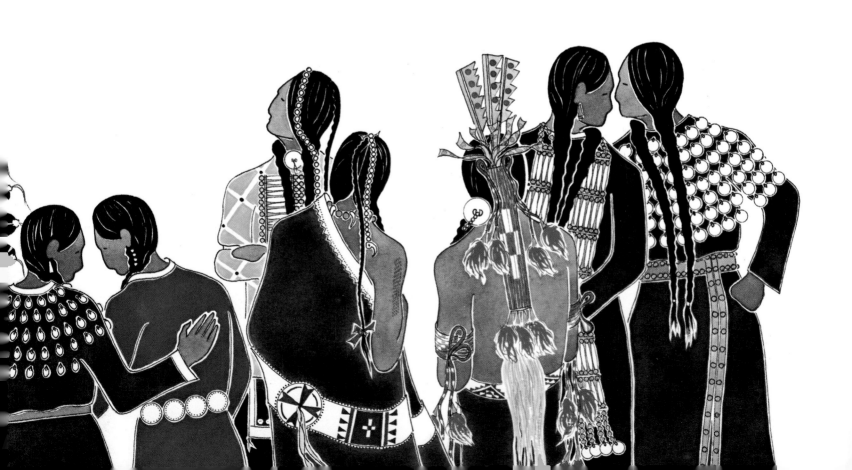

The young man was returning home when he saw his wife and child hurrying away from the camp. He was angry when he found out what had happened, and set out at once to bring them back.

Their trail led across rolling country. He followed all day, hearing the grasshoppers calling again and again from the sagebrush on every side. Evening was coming when he saw in the distance a painted tipi with smoke rising from a cooking fire.

The young man was surprised to see his son playing outside the tipi. When Calf Boy saw his father he ran to meet him. "I am glad you have come, Father. Mother has your meal ready." He took his father's hand and they went inside. The lodge was filled with the good smell of cooking. His wife placed a bowl of soup before him. "I am going home," she said. "I cannot live with your people. Do not follow us or you will be in great danger." "I love you," the young man said, "And wherever you and our son go, I am going too."

The young man awoke next morning looking up into the sky. The tipi was gone! There was nobody anywhere. Yet, it had not just been a dream, because he could see the circle in the dew-soaked grass where the tipi had stood, and the tracks of his wife and child leading away.

The young man followed their trail until he again came to the tipi. His son ran out to meet him.

"Mother does not want you to come any farther. Tomorrow she will make the rivers dry, but when you are thirsty, look for water in my tracks."

That evening his wife told him: "My people live beyond that distant high ridge. They know I am coming home. They are angry because your relatives were unkind to me. Do not follow any farther or they will kill you." But the young man replied: "It does not matter when I die. I shall not turn back. I do this because I love you both."

When his wife was asleep he buckled his belt through hers and wrapped her long hair around his arm.

Again the young man awoke alone. The only tracks in the
dew were those of a buffalo and her calf walking side by
side. While he was wondering about the tracks, a flock of
little birds flew around him excitedly: "They have gone
home! They have gone home!" He then knew that the tracks
were of his wife and child.

The tracks led toward the high ridge. Thin lines of trees
marked the winding rivers. They were dry, but just as Calf
Boy had told him, he found water in his hoof-prints in the
baked mud of the river-beds.

From the top of the high ridge the young man looked out in wonder over the multitude of the Buffalo Nation.

As he walked down toward them a calf came running out. "Father, go back! They will kill you! Go back!"

But the young man answered: "No, Son, I shall always stay with you and Mother."

"Then you must be brave," Calf Boy said. "My Grandfather is chief of the Buffalo Nation. Do not show fear or he will surely kill you. He will ask you to find me and Mother. But you think we all look alike! When he lines us up, you will know me because I shall flick my left ear. You will find Mother because I shall put a cockle-burr on her back. You must pick us out and then you will be safe. Be attentive!"

The old bull bellowed and charged out from the herd. The ground trembled under his thundering hoofs. He stopped just in front of the young man. He pawed the earth into dust clouds, hooked his horns into clumps of sagebrush and tossed them aside in anger. The young man stood still. He showed no fear.

"Ah, this Straight-up-Person has a strong heart," breathed the old bull. "By your courage you have saved yourself. Follow me."

The old bull led the way. The silent multitude parted and joined again behind. At the center was the painted tipi. The whole Buffalo Nation formed into radiating circles. The calves made the inner ring; the yearlings the next, the cows and bulls, all according to their ages.

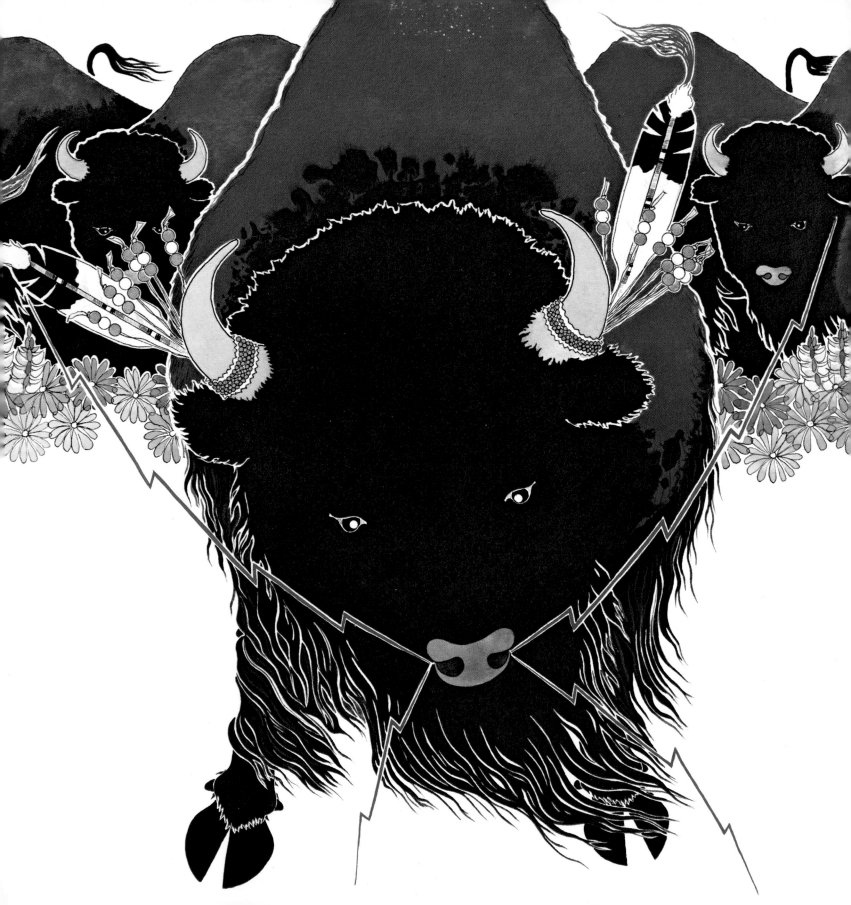

"Straight-up-Person," said the old bull in a voice which all could hear, "your relatives insulted my daughter. But you have come among us because you love your wife and child. Then *find* them! If you cannot, we shall trample you until not even a stain of your blood remains."

The young man passed in front of the little calves. They looked alike, but one flicked his ear as if troubled by a fly. He laid his hand on the calf's head. "My Son," he said, and a sound of surprise came from the multitude. "This must be a wonderful Person," they said.

He then walked around the circle formed by the cows. Again, they all looked alike, but he came to one with a cockle-burr on her back; "My Wife," he said. Once more a sound of surprise came from the Buffalo Nation: "Ah, he calls her 'Wife'."

"This Straight-up-Person loves his wife and little child," the old bull announced. "He was willing to die for them. We shall make him one of us. We shall all join in with our thoughts while we do this."

The young man was led inside the tipi and they tied the door shut. His only covering was a buffalo robe with the horns and hoofs attached.

For three days and nights the buffalo surrounded the tipi, filling the air with their continuous grunts and bellowing.

On the fourth day the bulls made a sudden rush and pushed the tipi over. They rolled and rolled the young man in a wallow until he was covered all over with dirt. They squeezed the breath from his body and breathed new breath into him. They licked him and rubbed against him until his man-smell was gone. He tried to stand but he could not. He felt the robe become a part of him. When the bulls heard him grunting they worked even harder, tumbling him over and over.

And at last, he stood up on his own four legs—a young buffalo bull.

That was a wonderful day! The relationship was made between the People and the Buffalo Nation; it will last until the end of time. It will be remembered that a brave young man became a buffalo because he loved his wife and little child. In return the Buffalo People have given their flesh so that little children, and babies still unborn, will always have meat to eat. It is the Creator's wish.

Mitakuye oyasin—We are all related.

Song of the Buffalo Bulls, from the Osage tribe:

I rise, I rise,
I, whose tread makes the earth rumble.

I rise, I rise,
I, in whose legs there is strength.

I rise, I rise,
I, who whips his back with his tail when in rage.

I rise, I rise,
I, in whose humped shoulder there is power.

I rise, I rise,
I, who shakes his mane when angered.

I rise, I rise,
I, whose horns are curved and sharp.